MOMMY AND DADDY ARE ISRAELITES TOO!

I KEEP THE LAWS, STATUTES AND COMMANDMENTS.

WHICH INCLUDES THE
DIETARY, CIVIL AND
MORAL LAWS

MOMMY AND DADDY KEEP THE CEREMONIAL LAWS TOO!

I WEAR FRINGES WITH A BORDER OF BLUE EVERY DAY.

I REMEMBER THE SABBATH DAY, AND KEEP IT HOLY.

Y	SATURDAY	S
	①	
Ⓐ	⑧	

NO BUYING, SELLING
OR COOKING.

I STUDY BIBLE VERSES.

I CELEBRATE HOLY DAYS,
NOT HOLIDAYS.

I EAT CLEAN FOODS ACCORDING TO THE DIETARY LAW.

I AM VERY SPECIAL.

I AM AN ISRAELITE.

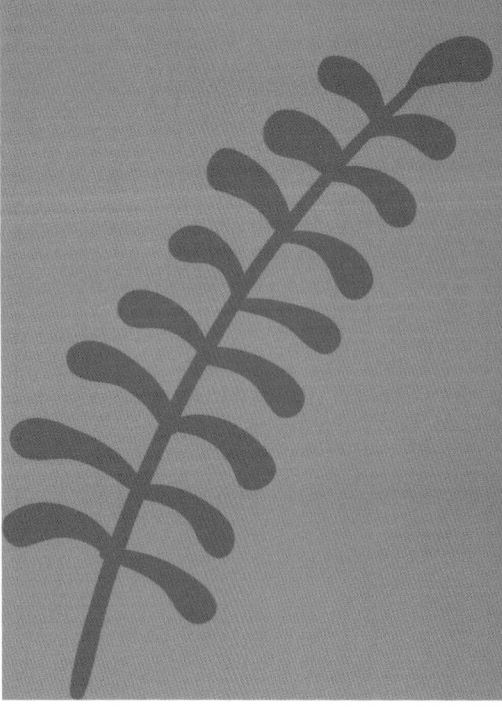

SHALOM

Printed in Great Britain
by Amazon